FRECKLY FEET
— and —
ITCHY KNEES

Michael Rosen
Illustrated by Sami Sweeten

PictureLions
An Imprint of HarperCollinsPublishers

For
Geraldine, Joe, Naomi, Eddie,
Laura and Isaac.

First published in Great Britain by William Collins Sons and Co Ltd in 1990
First published in Picture Lions in 1991
This edition published in 1992
Picture Lions is an imprint of the Children's Division,
part of HarperCollins Publishers Limited,
77-85 Fulham Palace Road, Hammersmith,
London W6 8JB

Printed in Great Britain

noses

I'm talking about noses
wet noses
warty noses
sleepy noses
when someone dozes

na na
na na
naah!

noses in hankies
noses in books
noses in crannies
noses in nooks

I'm talking about noses
noses at a flower show
the show is full of noses
noses in the tulips
noses in the roses

noses for wrinklir
noses for wigglin
noses for wagglin
noses for jiggling

noses that sneeze
noses that run
noses in the wind
noses in the sun

I'm talking about noses
noses on donkeys
mice's twitching noses
the noses on the elephants
looking more like hoses

noses underwater
blowing out bubbles
noses in a fight
in all kinds of trouble

dinosaur nose
Martian nose
eyes and nose
moustache and nose

I'm talking about noses
noses on the TV
puppets' big red noses
noses on photos
noses in posies

now give those noses a wipe
give those noses a blow
pull those noses hard
and watch those noses grow.

hands

I'm talking about hands
big hands
hot hands
hands on heads
handstands

wow!

hands in gloves
hands in a fist
hands in your pockets
hands that are kissed

ho ho!

I'm talking about hands
hands around bottles
sticky hands
hands around jam jars
hands around cans

hands that smack
hands that stroke
hands that point
hands that poke

hands for painting
hands for banging
hands for swinging
hands for hanging

I'm talking about hands
hands on the bongos
listen to your hands
beating out a rhythm
on the pots and pans

hands that clap
hands that grip
hands that shake
hands that slip

look at that giant's hands
look at that musician's hands
look at that monster's hands
look at that magician's hands

S-K-i-d

I'm talking about hands
hands in the cupboard
full up hands
hands making puddings
hands making flans

now give those hands a wave
right up in the sky
does that say hello?
or does it mean goodbye?

feet

I'm talking about feet
freckly feet
hairy feet
little feet
that babies eat

yum
yum

whee

feet in the mud
feet in the sand
feet in the water
feet in your hand

eek!

I'm talking about feet
skinny feet
fat feet
running feet
down the street

boo!

feet for climbing
feet for sliding
feet for dancing
feet for hiding

digging feet
crawling feet
skating feet
falling feet

I'm talking about feet
feet in the cold
feet in the heat
feet in a band
tapping out a beat

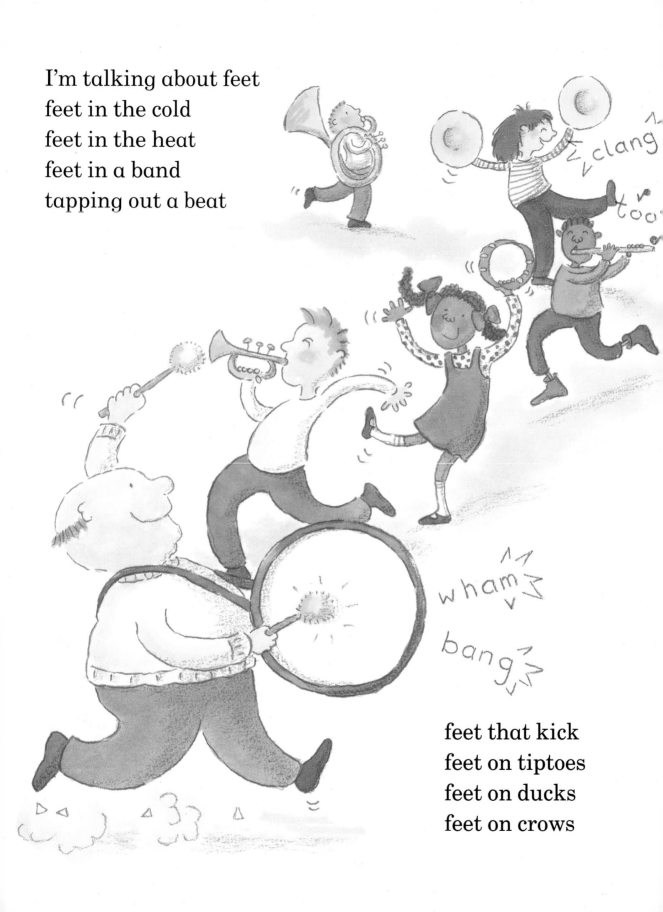

clang
too

wham
bang

feet that kick
feet on tiptoes
feet on ducks
feet on crows

look at that cat's feet
look at that dog's feet
look at that fly's feet
look at that frog's feet

I'm talking about feet, feet on a statue,
painted feet, feet looking messy
feet looking neat

now give those feet a tickle
stroke those little old feet
grab those feet and squeeze
and give those feet a treat

eyes

yum!

I'm talking about eyes
shut eyes
goggly eyes
greedy eyes
looking at pies

eyes up
eyes down
eyes to the side
and round and round

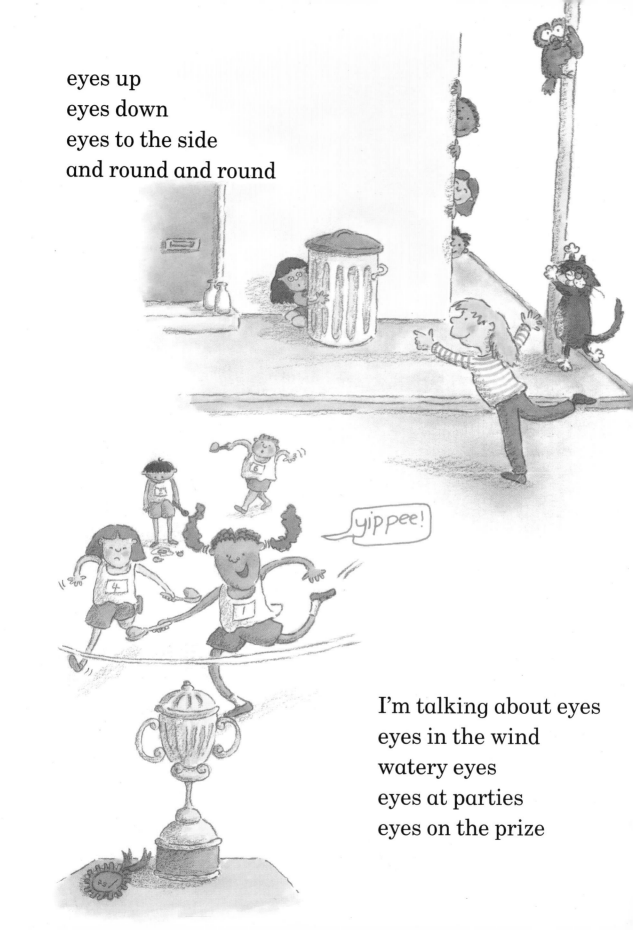

I'm talking about eyes
eyes in the wind
watery eyes
eyes at parties
eyes on the prize

eyes for snooping
eyes for spying
eyes for laughing
eyes for crying

eyes that watch
eyes that blink
eyes that hide
eyes that wink

I'm talking about eyes, big bushy eyebrows
covering up eyes
who broke the bowl?
eyes telling lies

eyes in glasses
eyes down the microscope
eyes in the night
looking through a telescope

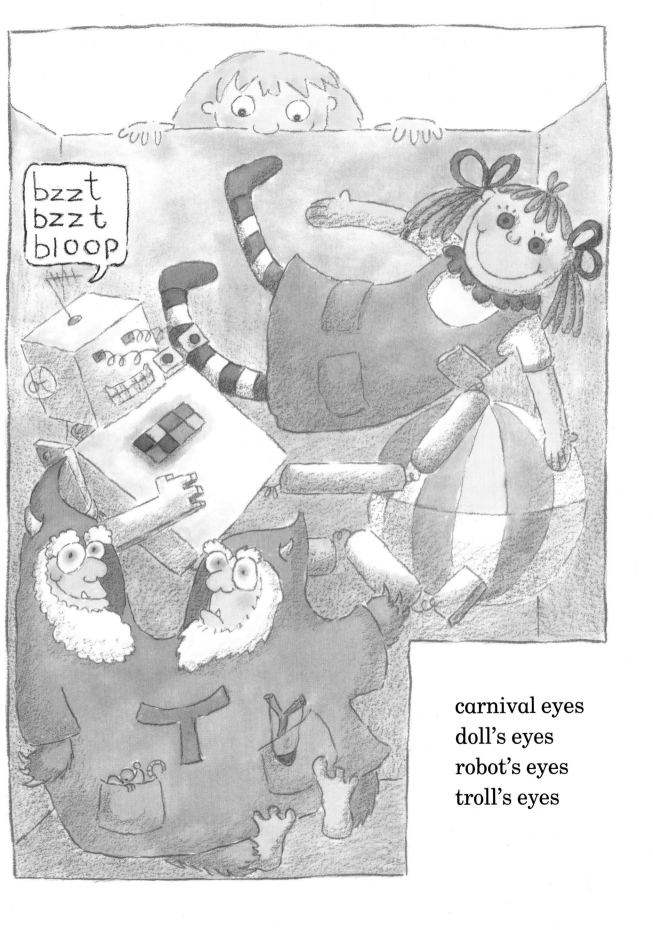

carnival eyes
doll's eyes
robot's eyes
troll's eyes

I'm talking about eyes
eyes on a mask
eyes on magpies
up in the mountains
golden eagle eyes

now give those eyes a rub
not too hard is best
now gently shut those eyes
and give yourself a rest

I'm talking about knees, knobbly knees
wobbly knees, itchy knees,
bitten by fleas

knees in a scrape, knees with blood on,
knees in jeans, knees with mud on

I'm talking about knees, knees at a dance,
knees in bed, knees in a row,
knees by your head

knees for bending
knees for running
knees for crouching
knees for drumming

knees that creak
knees that kneel
knees that shake
knees that peel

I'm talking about knees
knees in the wind
outdoor knees
frosty morning
knees that freeze

knees under the table
knees in the car
knees round the jam
knees in a jar

ghost's knees
fairy knees
goblin knees
hairy knees

zappo

I'm talking about knees, knees on a crab,
knees in trees, knees on an elephant,
little bees' knees

now give those knees a scratch
tickle those tickly knees
then rap out a neat little rhythm
then give those knees a squeeze

bellies

I'm talking about bellies
muscly bellies
mucky bellies
wobbly bellies
full of jellies

whee!

bellies on the beach
bellies up the mountain
bellies in the sun
bellies in the fountain

I'm talking about bellies
babies' bellies
dogs' bellies
dancers' bellies
wiggling on tellies

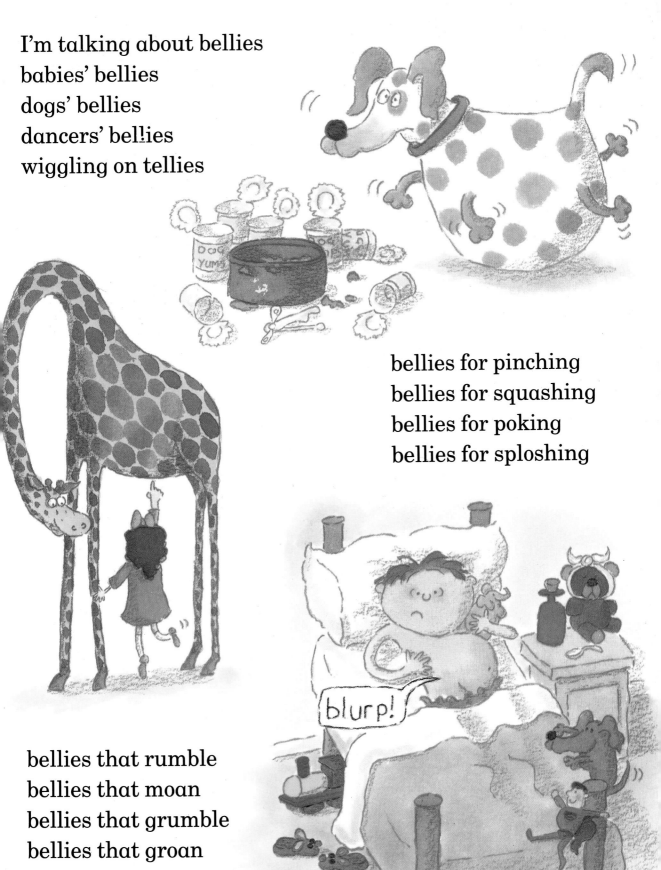

bellies for pinching
bellies for squashing
bellies for poking
bellies for sploshing

bellies that rumble
bellies that moan
bellies that grumble
bellies that groan

I'm talking about bellies
bellies on hippos
a really big belly
belly on a pig
very smelly belly

when
bellies bend over
bellies fold up
bellies lie flat
a place to put your cup

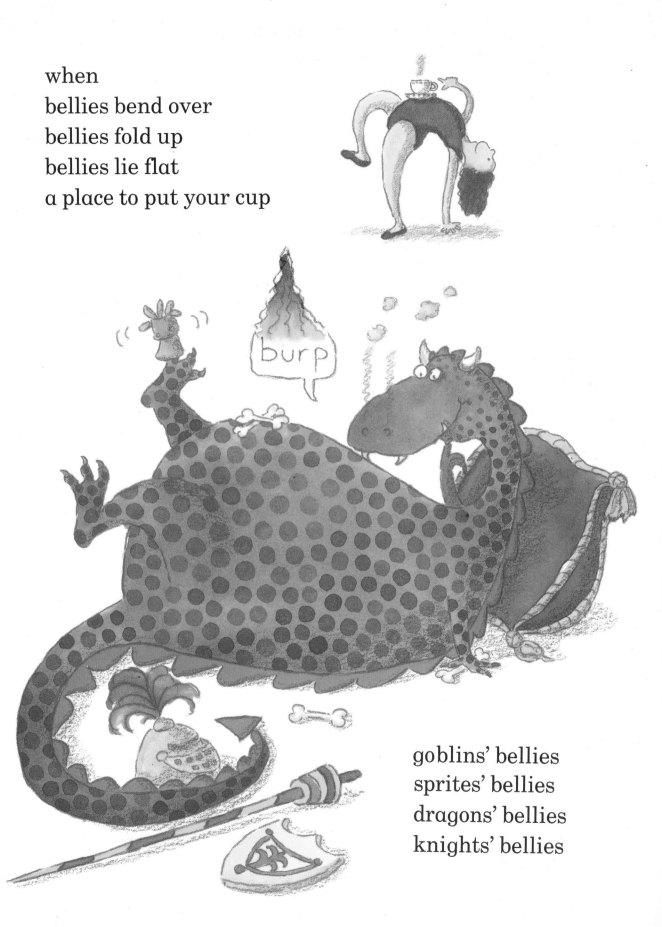

goblins' bellies
sprites' bellies
dragons' bellies
knights' bellies

Now there's one last thing to be done,
One last thing to be sung
We've got to get the
Noses going wiggle wiggle
Hands going jiggle jiggle
Feet going hop hop
Eyes going pop pop
Knees going knobble knobble
Bellies going wobble wobble

One more time: Wiggle wiggle
Jiggle Jiggle
Hop Hop
Pop Pop
Knobble knobble
Wobble wobble